Biographies

爭取民權
Martin Luther King Jr. and Rosa Parks

Anne Schraff

Development: Kent Publishing Services, Inc.
Design and Production: Signature Design Group, Inc.

Photo Credits: page 18, Flip Schukle/Black Star; page 54, Black Star Photos; page 60, Library of Congress/National Archives
Photo Credits: pages 94, 103, Library of Congress; page 125, The Rosa Parks Library and Museum

書　　名：爭取民權 Martin Luther King Jr. and Rosa Parks
作　　者：Anne Schraff
責　　編：黃家麗　王朴真
封面設計：張　毅
出　　版：商務印書館 (香港) 有限公司
香港筲箕灣耀興道 3 號東滙廣場 8 樓
http://www.commercialpress.com.hk
發　　行：香港聯合書刊物流有限公司
香港新界大埔汀麗路 36 號中華商務印刷大廈 3 字樓
印　　刷：中華商務彩色印刷有限公司
香港新界大埔汀麗路 36 號中華商務印刷大廈 14 字樓
版　　次：2012 年 10 月第 1 版第 1 次印刷

ISBN 978 962 07 1974 5
Printed in Hong Kong

CONTENTS 目錄

Part 2
Rosa Parks 羅莎・帕克斯

Publisher's Note
出版說明

繼出版以漫畫為主的 Graphic Biography 系列後，商務印書館推出 Biographies 系列。新系列從 TIME magazine 二十世紀最具影響力的名人中，精選了不同領域的十位名人，有科學家愛因斯坦、前美國總統羅斯福、民權領袖馬丁・路德・金，還有勇於突破局限的海倫・凱勒。

Biographies 系列經 Saddleback Educational Publishing 授權出版。本系列增加 Cultural Note（文化知識點），介紹相關社會背景；附帶練習題，可供讀者掌握生詞和英語語法點。

"淺顯易懂、啟發心智"是為特點。我們衷心希望，本系列能為初級英語程度的讀者提供閱讀和學習的樂趣。

商務印書館（香港）有限公司
編輯出版部

Usage Note
使用說明

Step 1

　　通讀傳記故事。遇到生詞可即時參考註釋。若不明白故事背景，可閱讀文化知識點。

Step 2

　　完成練習題。若未能回答練習題，或回答錯誤時，可再查閱傳記相關內容。通過練習熟悉生詞意義和用法，掌握語法知識。

Step 3

　　閱讀中英對照生詞表，檢查是否已掌握生詞。尚未掌握的生詞，可重新閱讀傳記相關部分。

Step 4

　　閱讀人物年表，重溫傳記故事。讀者可模仿年表，用簡單詞句概括重要事件，練習撮要技巧。

Step 5

　　延伸閱讀列出有參考價值的相關書籍，讀者可按興趣深入閱讀。

Part 1

Martin Luther King Jr.
馬丁・路德・金

A rebel 叛逆少年

By the 1950s, African Americans who lived in the South were segregated[1] in many ways. They had to ride in the back of buses and sit in the rear of theaters. Hotels and restaurants refused service.

African Americans of Montgomery, Alabama, boycotted[2] their segregated bus system. A young minister[3], Rev. Martin Luther King Jr., led them.

King led a peaceful struggle for civil rights. He endured beatings and imprisonment[4]. But he insisted on non-

1 be segregated, (passive) *v*: 被隔離
2 boycott, *v*: 聯合抵制
3 minister, *n*: 牧師
4 imprisonment, *n*: 監禁

violence. King succeeded in making all of America a more just[1] society.

Martin Luther King Jr. was born in Atlanta, Georgia, on January 15, 1929. His father, Martin Luther King Sr. was the assistant pastor[2] of Ebenezer Baptist Church*. A former sharecropper[3], King Sr. was a tough, strong man. The new baby was very healthy and was nicknamed M.L.

M.L.'s mother was Alberta Williams, a well educated and gentle woman. The Kings had three children. Willie Christina was older than M.L., and Alfred Daniel was younger. The family lived a happy life in a middle class, black neighbourhood[4] in Atlanta.

M.L. enjoyed playing baseball and flying kites with his friends. He rode his bicycle all around the neighborhood. Sometimes he went sliding down the

*Cultural Note

Ebenezer Baptist Church：埃比尼澤浸信會，馬丁・路德・金與其父都曾於此教會擔任神職。教會後來與其他幾處建築一同構成了現在的馬丁・路德・金國家歷史古蹟。

---

1 just, *adj*: 公正

2 pastor, *n*: 牧師

3 sharecropper, *n*: 佃農

4 neighbourhood, *n*: 社區，美 neighborhood

banister[1] of the family's two storey[2] house.

M.L.'s grandmother on his mother's side, Grandma Williams, was very close to M.L. She told the children stories and always supported them when they had problems.

When M.L. was a small boy, he was riding in the automobile with his father. Then, something happened that he never forgot. A white police officer pulled the car over[3] for going through a stop sign.

The police officer came to the window. He called M.L.'s father "boy," even though he was a grown man. M.L.'s father told the officer to treat him with the respect he deserved. M.L. was very proud of his father for standing up to[4] the white officer.

By the age of five, M.L. had a wonderful memory. He could recite long passages from the Bible. At six,

---

1 banister, *n*: 樓梯欄杆

2 storey, *n*: 樓層，美 story

3 pull over: 停車

4 stand up to: 反抗

M.L. began singing in church groups. Everybody loved the little boy with the strong, emotional[1] voice.

M.L.'s best friend during his early childhood was a white boy. The boy's father owned a nearby store.

The two boys played every day until the day it was time for them to start school. M.L. went to an all black school. His friend went to an all white school. But, M.L. hoped he and his friend could still play together after school.

Sadly, his friend told him their friendship was over because he was white and M.L. was African American. In the South, it was all right for very young children of different races to play together. But, when they reached school age, they were not supposed to be friends anymore.

---

1 emotional, *adj*: 有感染力

M.L. began to notice segregation more as he grew older. Black people could not use the parks or eat inside a restaurant. When M.L. went to a shoe store, he was told to try on shoes in the back.

Sometimes M.L. was disobedient[1], and his father whipped[2] him. When this happened, Grandma Williams would cry. This touched M.L.'s heart. He knew how much she loved him because she could not stand to see him punished.

When M.L. was twelve, his beloved grandmother died. He sobbed[3] as if his heart would break. She was his best friend in the world. M.L.'s parents told him Grandma Williams was in heaven now. Someday, they would all see her again.

After Grandma died, the King family moved. M.L. was becoming a teenager. He was growing more rebellious[4]. He continued to get whippings.

---

1 disobedient, *adj*: 不服從

2 whip, *v*: 鞭打

3 sob, *v*: 哭泣

4 rebellious, *adj*: 叛逆

Found God's calling 受到感召

As a teenager, Martin Luther King Jr. enjoyed wrestling[1], playing the piano, and listening to opera. Young Martin was a student at Booker T. Washington High School. He loved to read. Martin liked to eat too, especially fried chicken.

Martin loved his father. But he wanted to get away from him too. His father was a very strong person. Martin felt like he was standing in his shadow.

When Martin was in the 11th grade,

1 wrestle, *v*: 摔跤

he entered a speech contest. He won a prize and was very proud. But on the bus ride home from Dublin to Atlanta, Georgia, something ugly happened.

Some white people got on the bus. The driver told Martin and the other black students to get up and give their seats to the newcomers. Martin was furious[1]. But, he got up and stood in the aisle[2] on the long trip home.

In 1944 fifteen year old Martin was accepted to Atlanta's Morehouse College. The college also got him a summer job on a Connecticut tobacco[3] farm. Martin was thrilled[4] to have his first real job. He was happy too that it was far from home.

The work was hard. He was picking tobacco in the hot sun. But Martin felt free because he was away from home. On the weekends, Martin went into

---

1 furious, *adj*: 憤怒

2 aisle, *n*: 通道

3 tobacco, *n*: 煙草

4 thrilled, *adj*: 興奮

Hartford, Connecticut. There he saw movies and ate at diners.

Hartford was a northern city that was not segregated. Martin was delighted to be able to go wherever he wanted and sit where he pleased. He thought to himself that this is how it should be all over America.

When Martin started at Morehouse College, he did not know what he wanted to do in life. He did not want to follow in his father's footsteps[1] and be a minister. He thought he might be a doctor or a lawyer.

While going to college, Martin lived at home. He joined the glee club[2] and played football. But he soon found out that the college had very high standards.

He had gone all his life to all black elementary and high schools.

---

1 follow in one's footsteps: 步人後塵

2 glee club: 合唱團

Unfortunately, he was not well educated. Throughout the South at the time, education at black schools was poorer. There were fewer books and lower standards. Martin had to study very hard to catch up, but he did.

After attending Morehouse College for a while, Martin was surprised to find out he liked his religion classes. He admired some of the ministers who taught him. At the age of 17, Martin decided that he would be a minister after all.

When Martin's father heard his son's decision, he was delighted. This is what he always hoped for. Martin's father asked his son if he would like to preach a sermon[1] at the Ebenezer Baptist Church. Martin agreed and the people loved his sermon.

---

1 preach a sermon: 佈道

At the age of 18, Martin Luther King Jr. was appointed[1] Assistant Pastor at Ebenezer Church. Crowds of people came every Sunday to hear the young man with the strong voice preach from the heart.

Martin was still in college. During the summer, he worked as a laborer on the railroad. At 19, in 1948, Martin graduated from Morehouse College. He then went to Crozer Theological Seminary in Pennsylvania to get his Divinity degree[2]. Martin was one of six African American students at Crozer.

While attending Crozer, Martin Luther King Jr. began studying the philosophy of non violence. He read about Mohandas K. Gandhi* of India. Gandhi used non violence to lead India to independence from Great Britain.

*Cultural Note

Mohandas K. Gandhi：全名 Mohandas Karamchand Gandhi，莫罕達斯・卡拉姆昌德・甘地，印度民族主義運動和國大黨領袖，通過非暴力抵抗運動使印度脫離了英國的殖民統治。

1 be appointed, (passive) *v*: 被任命

2 Divinity degree: 神學學位

In June 1951 King received his degree. He was twenty-two-years old. After that, he was invited to attend Boston University in Massachusetts on a scholarship.

He fit in[1] well in Boston. He found many friends and a special young woman who was destined to be his wife.

Martin Luther King Jr. met Corretta Scott while attending school in Boston. They later married.
在波士頓求學時，馬丁・路德・金邂逅了科麗塔・斯科特，後來二人結婚。

1 fit in: 融入群體

Leadership started 始為領袖

Coretta Scott was a student at the New England Conservatory[1] of Music in Boston. She had a beautiful singing voice and dreams of a musical career. She was born on an Alabama farm. She had worked hard to get to the New England Conservatory.

A friend introduced Coretta Scott to Martin Luther King Jr. King fell in love with the lovely young woman right away. It took Scott a little longer to feel the same about King.

1 conservatory, *n*: 音樂學院

King told her that if they got married, she would have to forget about her musical career. He saw the role of a wife as homemaker[1] and mother. It was hard for Scott to give up her dream, but she did.

In June 1953 Coretta Scott married Martin Luther King Jr. The wedding was at her father's home in Marion, Alabama. King's father performed the ceremony[2].

The newlyweds[3] looked for a hotel for their wedding night. But no hotel in the area accepted black people. So they spent their wedding night at a friend's funeral parlor[4]. Later, King loved to joke about this.

The Kings returned to Boston while Martin finished his studies at Boston University. At the same time, Coretta completed her work at the

---

1 homemaker, *n*: 主婦

2 perform the ceremony: 主持儀式

3 newlyweds, *n*: 新婚夫婦

4 funeral parlor: 殯儀館

Conservatory. Then, King looked for a job as a minister. Now Dr. Martin Luther King Jr. with a Ph.D., he was offered a job as a pastor. The job was at Dexter Avenue Baptist Church in Montgomery, Alabama.

Coretta King did not want to move back to Alabama. She remembered the segregation as she grew up there. She liked the North better. She did not want to raise children in the segregated South. But, she told her husband that if that was what he wanted, she would accept it.

The Kings moved into a shabby[1] parsonage[2] at Dexter Avenue Baptist Church in April 1954. King worked hard at his first pastorate[3]. He visited the sick, prepared sermons[4], and attended meetings. The people loved him. He loved the work too. He felt he was really helping people.

---

1 shabby, *adj*: 破舊

2 parsonage, *n*: 牧師住宅

3 pastorate, *n*: 牧師任期

4 sermon, *n*: 講道

In November 1955 Yolanda Denise, was born. Her nickname was Yoki. Both Coretta and Martin were overjoyed to be parents of a healthy little girl. But, momentous[1] events were about to happen. These events would sweep the young minister into the spotlight[2].

On December 1, 1955, a weary[3] African American seamstress[4] named Rosa Parks was riding a Montgomery city bus home. She was asked to give up her seat to a white man who had just boarded the bus.

Black people were expected to immediately give up their seats if white people were standing. But, Parks did something unexpected and very courageous. She refused to get up. For that she was arrested and placed in jail.

The black people of Montgomery saw the arrest of Rosa Parks as a chance to

---

1 momentous, *adj*: 重大

2 sweep…into the spotlight: 使…成為焦點

3 weary, *adj*: 疲勞

4 seamstress, *n*: 女裁縫

do something about bus segregation. The United States Supreme Court had declared[1] school segregation unconstitutional[2].

Now, they hoped to take the case of Rosa Parks all the way to the Supreme Court. They hoped that segregation on public transportation would be declared unconstitutional too. But, they needed someone strong and brave to lead them in this fight.

Martin Luther King Jr. was chosen as president of the Montgomery Improvement Association (MIA)*. This group planned to call attention to the unfairness of bus segregation. They were going to do this by boycotting the Montgomery buses.

Rosa Parks went to court on charges[3] of refusing to obey a bus driver's order to yield her seat to a white man. The bus

*Cultural Note

Montgomery Improvement Association (MIA)：蒙哥馬利改進協會。成立於1955年，組織領袖為馬丁・路德・金。該組織在蒙哥馬利巴士聯合抵制運動中發揮了重要作用。

1 declare, *v*: 宣佈

2 unconstitutional, *adj*: 違憲

3 charge, *n*: 指控

boycott was scheduled for this day. Thirty thousand black people, from children to the aged, usually rode the Montgomery buses. On December 5 they were told to all stay home or find some other way to get where they were going.

The weather was cold in Montgomery that day. King wondered if people would be willing to walk to school and work. Early in the morning, he waited nervously to see if the buses would be empty of black riders as he hoped.

A great victory 偉大勝利

When Coretta and Martin Luther King Jr. saw the first bus coming down the street, they shouted with excitement. It was empty. All over Montgomery it was the same story. Black people carpooled[1] or walked. The bus boycott was a huge success.

Rosa Parks was convicted[2] and fined ten dollars. The conviction[3] would be appealed[4]. Maybe it would go all the way to the federal courts. Hopes were high that bus segregation could be ended and

1 carpool, *v*: 共乘
2 be convicted, (passive) *v*: 被判有罪
3 conviction, *n*: 定罪
4 appeal, *v*: 上訴

called unconstitutional. Meanwhile, the bus boycott would continue.

King and the other members of MIA made some demands as conditions to end the bus boycott. Black drivers had to be hired where the riders were mostly African American. Seating on the bus had to be first come, first served[1]. If a black person had a seat, he or she could not be forced to give it up to someone who boarded the bus later.

Finally, many white bus drivers were treating their black passengers rudely. Elderly black women were called "girl,"and mature black men were called "boy." This had to stop. Black riders wanted to be treated with the same courtesy[2] as white people.

Many white people in Montgomery blamed King for the bus boycott. The bus company was losing money. White

---

1 first come, first served: 先到先得

2 treat with courtesy: 以禮相待

businesses in town were losing their many black customers. King received threatening phone calls.

Then, King was driving thirty miles per hour in a twenty-five miles per hour zone. The police stopped him. Instead of just giving him a ticket, the police threw him in jail with criminals. When many black people protested around the jail, King was freed until his trial[1] date.

But the harassment[2] continued. Everyday, hate mail came to the parsonage. Coretta King was worried about the safety of their baby. She dreaded[3] the ringing of the phone because so many of the calls were threats.

King himself feared that something violent might happen. He told his followers that no matter what happened, they could not answer

---

1 trial, *n*: 審判

2 harassment, *n*: 騷擾

3 dread, *v*: 懼怕

violence with violence[1]. King looked at his wife and baby, and a terrible thought went through his mind. He realized that he might lose them if angry whites attacked the house.

King was so worried about his family that he felt he could not go on as president of the MIA. He prayed for strength. Then, he felt as if a voice were telling him he had to stand up for justice no matter what.

On January 30, 1956, the bus boycott was still on. King was at a church meeting when someone came to him with dreadful[2] news. His house had been bombed. Coretta and his baby daughter were inside when it happened.

King rushed home to find his family unhurt. Only quick thinking saved them. Coretta King heard a thud[3] on the front porch[4] and ran to the back. The

---

1 answer violence with violence: 以暴制暴

2 dreadful, *adj*: 可怕

3 thud, *n*: 重擊聲

4 porch, *n*: 門廊

thud was a bundle of dynamite sticks[1]. The dynamite exploded and ripped out[2] the front window. Glass was sprayed[3] all over.

News of the bombing spread through the black community. The people were angry. A large crowd gathered before King's damaged house.

Some of them talked about getting the people who did this. But King made a powerful sermon. He told them they had to love even the people who committed violence against them. Then, King led everybody in singing the old hymn "Amazing Grace." Violence had been averted[4].

The business people of Montgomery were losing a lot of money from the bus boycott. So, they demanded action. The county Grand Jury indicted Martin Luther King Jr. and the other MIA

---

1 dynamite sticks: 炸藥棒

2 rip out: 炸開

3 spray, *v*: 飛濺

4 be averted, (passive) *v*: 被避免

members. They were indicted[1] for the crime of running an illegal boycott.

When King came to trial he was convicted. But King appealed. King's lawyers argued that the segregation of buses was illegal in the first place.

On June 4, 1956, the federal court agreed. When the case went to the Supreme Court*, bus segregation was outlawed[2]. The MIA won a great victory.

*Cultural Note

Supreme Court： 美國最高法院，於 1789 年成立。由一名首席大法官及六名大法官組成。七名法官都須由美國總統提名，並經美國參議院多數表決贊同方可任命。

1 be indicted, (passive) *v*: 被起訴

2 be outlawed, (passive) *v*: 被宣告非法

Escaped from death 死裏逃生

In December 1956, Martin Luther King Jr. boarded a bus in Montgomery, Alabama. The white bus driver gave him a friendly welcome. King sat where he wanted.

Because of his success in ending bus segregation, King became famous all over the country. He was even known around the world. Newspapers from foreign countries wrote articles about him. He was the brave young black minister who stood up for[1] his people.

1 stand up for: 捍衛

On February 18, 1957, King appeared on the cover of Time Magazine. There was a big story about him. He was only twenty eight years old. Already, he had changed history.

Many black leaders came to Montgomery, Alabama to talk about the next step in advancing civil rights[1]. Buses were desegregated[2] but life was still far from equal for African Americans. In many places, they were discouraged from voting. Restaurants and hotels excluded them.

The Southern Christian Leadership Conference (SCLC)* was founded. The goal was to use black churches to coordinate[3] civil rights activities. King was chosen as president of the SCLC. The first thing on the agenda was the registration of new black voters.

*Cultural Note

Southern Christian Leadership Conference (SCLC)：南方基督教領袖會議，創建於 1957 年，馬丁・路德・金任會長，是以南方基督教會為主的黑人民權組織，在美國民權運動中發揮了重要作用。

1 civil rights: 公民權

2 be desegregated, (passive) *v*: 被廢除種族隔離

3 coordinate, *v*: 協調

In October 1957 Martin Luther King III was born. In the same year, King received the National Association for Colored People's highest award. The award is called the Spingarn Medal*. He was honored for what he had done for African Americans.

But many white people were still angry with King for his work. They wanted the South to remain segregated. They were happy with the way things had been when black people stayed "in their place." That meant segregated and denied[1] equal opportunities.

In 1958 King was walking to the Montgomery County courthouse[2] with a friend. His friend had to deal with a legal matter[3] there. King was going along to give him support.

As King and his friend reached the courthouse door, a police officer yelled

*Cultural Note

Spingarn Medal：斯平加恩獎章，由全國有色人種協進會頒發，創始人為全國有色人種協進會的董事長斯平加恩。1914 年開始每年獎勵一位卓有成就的黑人。

1 denied, *adj*: 不被承認

2 courthouse, *n*: 法院大樓

3 legal matter: 法律問題

at King to stop. They told King he had no business in the courthouse. When King tried to explain his position, he was placed under arrest[1].

King's arms were yanked[2] behind his back. He was dragged down the sidewalk. Coretta King saw it happen. But when she tried to help her husband the police threatened her with arrest too.

King was taken to the police station. Then he was led down a long hall to a cell. Before he was shoved[3] in, King was grabbed by the throat[4] by one of the officers. Then he was violently thrown into the cell.

Martin Luther King Jr. was a famous man. But the officers who arrested him did not know him. They thought he was just an ordinary black man.

---

1 arrest, *n*: 逮捕

2 be yanked, (passive) *v*: 被猛拉

3 be shoved, (passive) *v*: 被猛推

4 be grabbed by the throat: 被掐住頸部

Black people were not supposed to talk back to white officers. When they told him to stay out of the courthouse he should have obeyed them. That was what they believed. But later on they found out whom they had arrested.

The Montgomery officials quickly released[1] him. King told the world how he had been treated. He made the point that this was how most black men were treated in the South. This, he said, had to change.

Martin Luther King Jr. wrote a book titled *Stride[2] Toward Freedom: The Montgomery Story*. In the book, he told the story of the bus boycott. He explained how bus segregation had been brought to an end.

In September 1958 King was signing autographs[3] in a department store in

1 release, *v*: 釋放

2 stride, *v*: 大步走

3 autograph, *n*: 親筆簽名

New York. A mentally ill black woman ran up to him. She stabbed[1] him with a razor-sharp[2] letter opener. The blade[3] plunged[4] deeply into King's chest. King was rushed to a hospital.

The surgeons who operated on him found the blade very close to the aorta[5]. The aorta is the largest artery[6] in the body. It was so close that any movement could have killed King.

The doctors worked on King for three hours. They removed a rib[7] and his breastbone[8] to get at[9] the blade. Finally it was safely removed. King was saved.

---

1 stab, *v*: 刺
2 razor-sharp, *adj*: 鋒利
3 blade, *n*: 刀刃
4 plunge, *v*: 插入
5 aorta, *n*: 主動脈
6 artery, *n*: 動脈
7 rib, *n*: 肋骨
8 breastbone, *n*: 胸骨
9 get at: 足夠取出

Letter from a jail 監獄來信

In late 1959 Martin Luther King Jr. became co-pastor of Ebenezer Baptist Church in Atlanta with his father. Almost immediately, his enemies were at work.

He was indicted by the Montgomery Grand Jury back in Alabama for tax fraud[1]. The people who hated him had bombed his house and had him arrested. Since that did not stop him, now they hoped to prove he was dishonest and destroy him in this way.

1 tax fraud: 稅務欺詐

King never had much money. Most of what he earned he gave to the SCLC. His income as co pastor of his church was $6000 a year. He drove an old Pontiac and lived in a small rented house. He had no money to pay back taxes and penalties[1]. He also knew he had done nothing wrong.

King's friends hired some good lawyers to defend him. They paid the lawyers because King could not.

On Monday, May 23, 1960, King stood trial[2]. King looked at the twelve white jurors[3]. He wondered how they could believe a black man. He thought surely he would be convicted. But the jury found him "not guilty." King was deeply touched.

With the tax problem out of the way, King turned his attention to a new cause. He wanted to desegregate eating

---

1 penalty, *n*: 罰金

2 stand trial: 受審

3 juror, *n*: 陪審員

places. For decades, black people could not sit in restaurants or at lunch counters. In the South, they could only be served on paper plates out the back doors.

In Atlanta, Georgia, King worked with a group of black college students. They were conducting a sit-in[1] at Rich's Department Store lunch counter. King was arrested and taken to jail.

While King was there, the authorities discovered an old traffic violation[2] of King's. They used that to transfer him to a tough prison for serious criminals. The prison was called Reidsville.

He was taken to Reidsville in the middle of the night in handcuffs[3] and chains. He was thrown into a dirty, cockroach-infested[4], bitter-cold cell. King became ill and feverish. He was frightened.

---

1 sit-in, *n*: 靜坐抗議

2 traffic violation: 交通違規

3 handcuff, *n*: 手銬

4 cockroach-infested, *adj*: 蟑螂成群

Senator[1] John F. Kennedy found out what had happened. He was running for president of the United States. He intervened[2], and King was immediately released. From then on, King and Kennedy were friends.

On January 30, 1961, Dexter Scott, the King's third child, was born.

In the spring, college students were going into the South to end pockets[3] of segregation. They were called Freedom Riders. Martin Luther King Jr. took up their cause, even though he was threatened by angry white mobs[4].

The King's fourth child, Albertina, was born. King tried to spend more time with his family. He had been so busy that he worried he was neglecting them.

In April 1963 Dr. Martin Luther King Jr. joined civil rights demonstrations in

---

1 senator, *n*: 參議員

2 intervene, *v*: 介入

3 pocket, *n*: 小地區

4 mob, *n*: 暴民

Birmingham, Alabama. This city was one of the most strictly segregated in the South. The police commissioner[1], Theophilus "Bull" Connor, was known for being tough.

King was arrested in one of the first protest marches. He was put in a small, dark cell. He had no mattress[2] and no bedding. President John Kennedy*. learned what happened. He called the Birmingham authorities. Then, King received a mattress and a blanket[3]. He was also allowed to shower and shave and talk to his wife on the phone.

King wanted to write down what he was feeling, but he had no paper. He wrote on scraps[4] of toilet paper and in the margins of old newspapers.

The words he wrote became a famous essay that was published all over the world. It was called "Letter from a

*Cultural Note

President John Kennedy：通常稱為 President John F.Kennedy，即約翰・F・堅尼地總統（1917-1963）。他是美國第 35 任總統，也是美國歷史上首任登上總統寶座的天主教徒。於 1963 年不幸遭暗殺身亡。

1 police commissioner: 警察局長
2 mattress, *n*: 牀墊
3 blanket, *n*: 毯子
4 scrap, *n*: 碎片

Birmingham Jail." King said in the letter that black people were tired of waiting for their rights.

King was freed, and there were more large demonstrations. Children and adults were attacked by the police with high pressure hoses[1]. Bull Connor's men beat the people with clubs[2] and fists. All this violence was shown on television. The nation was shocked.

The authorities of Birmingham were very ashamed about what had happened. They agreed to desegregate the downtown stores. They also agreed to hire more African Americans and free all of the protesters who were still in jail. King had won another big victory in the civil rights crusade[3].

---

1 high pressure hose: 高壓水槍

2 club, *n*: 棍

3 crusade, *n*: 改革運動

I have a dream 我有一個夢想

Requests came from all over America for Martin Luther King Jr. to speak. He addressed thousands of people in Chicago, Los Angeles, and Detroit.

At the time, President John F. Kennedy was about to introduce major civil rights legislation[1]. It would outlaw segregation on interstate[2] transportation. It would also force school integration[3].

King believed this law would be of great benefit to black people. In fact, it

1 legislation, *n*: 立法

2 interstate, *adj*: 州際

3 integration, *n*: 種族融合

would be beneficial to all Americans who wanted to live in a more just society. But a dramatic event was needed to bring the need for this law to America.

A. Philip Randolph came up with an idea. He was the founder of the largest black union in America, the Brotherhood of Sleeping Car Porters*. He urged[1] a massive[2] march on Washington, D.C.

Black people and those whites who also wanted justice would take part in the march. King liked the idea. But many white people were afraid such a big march would lead to violence. Some people in the United States government thought Martin Luther King Jr. was a dangerous man. They felt he was a threat to America.

*Cultural Note

Brotherhood of Sleeping Car Porters：臥車列車員兄弟會。成立於 1925 年，是美國第一個黑人工會。其首任以及第二任的會長，後來都成為美國民權運動的領袖。

1 urge, *v*: 竭力主張
2 massive, *adj*: 大型

J. Edgar Hoover was the head of the Federal Bureau of Investigation (FBI) at the time. He feared that Communists, who were spreading revolution around the world, were behind King.

Communism was considered a real threat to the free world. In many countries, Communists undermined[1] the government by stirring up[2] minority groups. Hoover believed that was what King was doing. Hoover suspected that King was a Communist himself.

Hoover had a list of Americans he believed were enemies of the country. King was on this list. So, Hoover planted[3] listening devices[4] in King's offices.

He hoped to find proof of King working with Communists. He also planted listening devices in hotels were King stayed. He was sure he would be able to hear King

---

1 undermine, *v*: 逐漸破壞

2 stir up: 煽動

3 plant, *v*: 埋設

4 listening device: 竊聽器

and other Communists talking about overthrowing[1] the American government.

Hoover feared that the march on Washington might be the beginning of Communist-sponsored[2] unrest[3] and violence in America. He thought it was going to lead to a revolution.

On August 28, 1963, about one hundred thousand African Americans and whites gathered. They were at the Lincoln Memorial in Washington, D.C. Another one hundred fifty thousand were on their way in trains, buses, cars, and planes.

In the end, over two hundred thousand African Americans and sixty thousand whites heard Martin Luther King Jr. speak. He delivered the most famous speech he ever made. It has become one of the most celebrated speeches in American history.

---

1 overthrow, *v*: 推翻

2 sponsored, *adj*: 資助

3 unrest, *n*: 騷亂

King spoke about a dream he had for America where all people, regardless of their color, creed[1], or background would enjoy equality. The speech was called the "I Have A Dream" address[2].

King's powerful voice and his emotional delivery[3] left the crowd with wild joy. Many wept and others cheered. President Kennedy invited King and other civil rights leaders to the White House to celebrate. It seemed as if the speech had united everybody in America in the cause of justice for all.

J. Edgar Hoover was not happy. He watched King grow more popular. He still believed King was a Communist agent. Martin Luther King Jr. was a Christian minister with a strong faith in God. Communists do not believe in God, but this did not convince[4] Hoover.

---

1 creed, *n*: 信仰

2 address, *n*: 演講

3 delivery, *n*: 演講方式

4 convince, *v*: 說服

Hoover never found a link between King and the Communists. He did, however, find something that he hoped would destroy King's reputation.

After the successful march on Washington, King and his friends celebrated at a party at the Willard Hotel in Washington. The FBI had listening devices in the room. They picked up sounds of a very lively party.

Hoover sent copies of the tape to President Kennedy and other government agencies. He also sent a copy to Coretta King. Hoover believed the tape showed King partying with other women. But Coretta King dismissed[1] the whole thing.

1963 had been a year of challenge and triumph for King. Before the year ended, it would be a year of tragedy.

---

1 dismiss, *v*: 不理會

A Nobel laureate 諾獎得主

On September 15, 1963, a monstrous[1] act of violence erupted[2] from the racial hatred[3] in Birmingham, Alabama.

Birmingham's Sixteenth Street Baptist Church had been a starting place for many of the successful civil rights marches. On this Sunday morning, four little girls were getting ready to sing in the choir. Then, someone dynamited the church. The children all died. Martin Luther King Jr. admitted to being as near to despair[4] as he had ever been.

1 monstrous, *adj*: 駭人聽聞

2 erupt, *v*: 爆發

3 racial hatred: 種族仇恨

4 despair, *n*: 絕望

On November 22 another terrible blow[1] fell. King had grown very close to President John F. Kennedy. He saw the young president as a sincere ally[2] in the cause of civil rights. Now, the news bulletin from Dallas, Texas, announced the assassination of President Kennedy. In his shock and grief, King told his wife that he felt sure the same fate would befall[3] him, too.

President Lyndon Johnson* succeeded Kennedy. Johnson pledged[4] to make the civil rights bill into law.

*Cultural Note

President Lyndon Johnson：通常稱為 President John B. Johnson，即靈登・B・約翰森總統，美國第36任總統。美國歷史上有四位總統曾經擔任過眾議院議員、參議院議員、副總統和總統全部四個職位，約翰森總統是其中之一。

In 1964 Martin Luther King Jr. was awarded the Nobel Peace Prize. King went to Oslo, Norway, to receive the prize. He pledged to give the entire cash amount to the cause of civil rights. He said in his Nobel address that the prize was not a personal triumph. Instead, he said, it was a recognition of all who struggled for justice.

1 blow, *n*: 打擊
2 ally, *n*: 盟友
3 befall, *v*: 降臨
4 pledge, *v*: 承諾

In 1965 a civil rights march from Selma to Montgomery, Alabama, became a catastrophe[1]. Hundreds of marchers were confronted by[2] state troopers.

The troopers plunged into the crowd on horses. They beat and trampled[3] the people. King was not in this march. But he led another march from Selma to Montgomery. The publicity helped President Johnson turn the 1965 Civil Rights Act into law.

At this time, the United States was fighting a war in South Vietnam. The U.S. wanted to stop the spread of Communism in Asia. Many Americans opposed the war.

Thousands of U.S. soldiers along with hundreds of thousands of Vietnamese had already died. Even though President Johnson firmly believed in the war,

---

1 catastrophe, *n*: 災難

2 be confronted by: 面對

3 trample, *v*: 踩踏

Martin Luther King Jr. came out against it. He said it was a waste of precious lives. Also, the money would be better spent easing poverty[1] in America.

King was criticized for opposing the war in Vietnam. Even some of his friends were upset with him. But, King continued to speak against the war. He also focused his attention on poverty in the northern United States.

Coretta Scott and Martin Luther King Jr. moved into a shabby old railway carriage[2]. The car was in a poverty stricken neighborhood of Chicago. It was on Chicago's run down west side.

In that area, there was no sign of trees or lawns. The house the Kings lived in had two bedrooms, a kitchen, and bathroom. The gas stove[3] was broken and the ceiling and walls were crumbling[4].

---

1 ease poverty: 減少貧困

2 railway carriage: 火車車廂，美 railroad car

3 gas stove: 煤氣爐

4 crumbling, *adj* : 剝落

Many Chicagoans lived like this. King said it was not right. Even poor people deserve decent[1] places to live, he argued. The people who lived in these shacks[2] paid high rent. King said they should refuse to pay another cent until the houses were made livable.

In December 1967 King planned a large demonstration to show his commitment[3] to the poor of America. He wanted to bring thousands of poor people to the Washington monument.

He wanted a tent city[4] to be built. The tent city would demonstrate that these people lacked suitable homes for themselves and their children.

King's plans to lead a poor people's march on Washington and his continued criticism of the war in Vietnam raised old accusations[5] against

---

1 decent, *adj*: 像樣
2 shack, *n*: 棚屋
3 commitment, *n*: 投身
4 tent city: 帳篷城
5 accusation, *n*: 譴責

him. The war in Vietnam was to stop Communism. King wanted to pull out[1]. President Johnson was angry at King's comments. King's popularity sunk from its former high level.

But Martin Luther King Jr. continued with his plans. He was interrupted by another labour strike in Memphis, Tennessee.

Sanitation workers in Memphis called on Matin Luther King Jr. to help them get better wages and working conditions.

孟菲斯的清潔工人懇請馬丁・路德・金幫助提高工人薪酬和改善工作環境。

---

1 pull out : 退出

CHAPTER 9

Last speech 最後的演説

Most of the sanitation workers in Memphis* were black. They received low pay for dirty, dangerous work. There were no normal worker benefits.

Two workers were crushed to death[1] in a dustcart[2] in February 1968. Their families were left with nothing. This tragedy called attention to the fact that the workers had no medical benefits. They had no unemployment compensation[3] with survivor benefits[4]

*Cultural Note

Memphis：孟菲斯市，位於美國田那斯州的西南角，美國主要河流密西西比河的沿岸。該處最早為美洲原住民定居地區，1795 年由西班牙人收購。

1 be crushed to death: 被壓死
2 dustcart, *n*: 垃圾車，[美] garbage truck
3 unemployment compensation: 失業救濟金
4 survivor benefits: 遺屬撫恤金

either. The sanitation workers asked for better wages[1] and conditions. But when they were turned down, they formed a union.

The sanitation workers of Memphis were on strike. But they were getting nowhere. The city planned to fire them all. In desperation, they called on Martin Luther King Jr. They wanted him to lend his prestige[2] to their cause.

King's staff told him he had no time to get involved in the Memphis strike. King had promised to make many speeches all over the South for civil rights. There was no time to visit Memphis. But, in spite of this, King decided to go.

He told his staff that if he was fighting for poor people, how could he ignore these sanitation workers who had so little?

---

1 wages, [pl], *n*: 工資

2 prestige, *n*: 威望

Martin Luther King Jr. planned to make a quick trip to Memphis. Then he would leave town and resume[1] his speaking tour. He thought when he got there that he would be talking to a small crowd. But when he arrived at the hall there were fifteen thousand people waiting for him.

King made a powerful speech for the sanitation workers. He promised them that if the city had not yet met their just demands, he would come back in ten days. If he came back, he would lead a protest march on their behalf.

Memphis did not meet the demands of the union. So, on Thursday, March 28, King and other civil rights leaders led a march.

King had always insisted that all his marches be peaceful, but trouble

---

1 resume, *v*: 重新開始

quickly broke out. Young Memphis African Americans in the march started shouting. They committed vandalism[1] along the march route.

The police charged in and the whole demonstration was a disaster. King was crushed by the turn of events. He planned another march. He insisted that this time it would be nonviolent.

On April 3 King returned to Memphis. He gave a strong speech asking for a nonviolent march. Those who heard him speak said they never heard him speak so eloquently[2].

The march was scheduled for April 5. King was sure it would be peaceful and effective. The sanitation workers would finally receive the justice they deserved.

Everything seemed to be falling into place. The local judge approved the

---

1 vandalism, *n*: 故意破壞

2 eloquently, *adv*: 有說服力

march. King met with some young black men who promised to cooperate with him.

It was 6:00 on the evening of April 4. King and a fellow minister and civil rights activist, Rev. Ralph Abernathy, were getting ready. They were about to leave their room in the Lorraine Motel in Memphis. King went out onto the balcony. He began talking to some people gathered below.

There was a lodging house[1] across the street from the motel. Inside one of the rooms was an ex-convict[2] white man. His name was James Earl Ray.

Ray held in his hand a rifle[3]. He was a drifter[4] who hated black people. Ray's life was a bitter failure. He was filled with anger.

---

1 lodging house: 分房出租的公寓，美 rooming house

2 ex-convict, *n*: 前科犯

3 rifle, *n*: 步槍

4 drifter, *n*: 流浪漢

As King stood on the balcony, a rifle shot came from the direction of the lodging house. The bullet hit King in the lower right jaw[1]. His jawbone[2] was shattered. Then, the bullet drove into his neck. It tore major blood vessels[3]. King's spinal cord[4] was cut.

Martin Luther King Jr. lay on the floor of the balcony. Friends tried desperately to stop the blood pouring from his terrible wounds.

No one knew that King's powerful speech in Memph would be his last.
沒有人想到金在孟菲斯發表的動人演說將會是最後的演說

---

1 jaw, *n:* 下巴
2 jawbone, *n*: 下顎骨
3 blood vessel: 血管
4 spinal cord: 脊髓

The spirit never dies 精神永存

An ambulance rushed King to St. Joseph's Hospital. Paramedics[1] worked on him until they reached the emergency room. There, doctors gave him oxygen and did all they could. It was not enough. He was beyond help.

Martin Luther King Jr. died at 7:05 p.m., April 4, 1968.

April 7 was named a national day of mourning[2]. From all over the world came words of shock and sorrow.

1 paramedic, *n*: 護理人員

2 mourning, *n*: 哀悼

Coretta King comforted[1] her four young children with the religious faith that had been the center of the King home. Coretta King assured her children their father was in Heaven. She told them that they would see him again.

On April 5, Coretta King and her three oldest children marched in the sanitation workers demonstration as her husband promised he would. The city of Memphis immediately accepted all the demands of the union. The sanitation workers at last had justice.

King's body lay in Atlanta where thousands of people filed past the coffin[2]. The funeral was conducted at Ebenezer Baptist Church. There, famous people shared pews[3] with King's many friends. King's body was placed in a farm cart. It was pulled by two mules to the cemetery where he was buried.

---

1 comfort, *v*: 安慰

2 coffin, *n*: 靈柩，美 casket

3 pew, *n*: 教堂的靠背長椅

On King's tombstone were placed words from one of his greatest speeches: "Free at last, free at last, thank God Almighty[1] I'm free at last."

Two months after King's death, James Earl Ray was arrested in London, England. His fingerprints were found on the murder weapon. At his trial he pleaded[2] guilty to killing Martin Luther King Jr. Later, he denied it. He was convicted and sentenced to 99 years in prison. He died in prison in 1994.

After King's death, the 1968 Civil Rights Act* passed. It made housing discrimination illegal. A year after King's death, his widow began to build a center. It was called the Martin Luther King Jr. Center for Nonviolent Social Change. It was located in Atlanta.

The Center's purpose was to spread King's ideals. In January 1982 it

*Cultural Note

1968 Civil Rights Act：1968 年美國民權法案，由靈登・B・約翰森總統簽署。此法案旨在保障美國人，不論種族、信仰，都有平等的住房權力。

1 God Almighty: 全能的上帝

2 plead, *v*: 辯護

opened. The body of Martin Luther King Jr. was brought there. King's remains[1] now rest at the Freedom Hall exhibit.

After King's death, cities, schools, and public buildings all over the United States were named for him. Martin Luther King Jr.'s birthday is now a federal holiday. Each year there are parades[2] and public events honoring his legacy[3].

The true legacy of Martin Luther King Jr. lies in how he changed the social fabric of America. When his struggle began there was rampant[4] segregation in the South. African Americans could not freely use public transportation or private and public facilities of any kind.

King led a nonviolent movement to erase the blight[5] of racial segregation.

---

1 remains, [pl], *n*: 遺骸

2 parade, *n*: 遊行

3 legacy, *n*: 遺產

4 rampant, *adj*: 猖獗

5 blight, *n*: 破壞

During his life, he insisted on giving credit to many people. He credited the hundreds and thousands of black and white civil rights workers who made his dream for equality come true.

But history will remember that the leadership of Martin Luther King Jr. was a powerful force. It made America a more just society for everyone. King lived for just thirty-nine years. But, because of him, millions enjoy a better, more just life, and a more promising future.

In 1986 President Ronald Reagan declared January 18 as a national holiday honouring Martin Luther King Jr. His image appears on over 100 stamps in nations around the world.

1986 年，為紀念馬丁・路德・金，羅諾德・雷根總統宣佈 1 月 18 日為美國全國的假日。印有馬丁・路德・金形象的郵票在一百多個國家發行。

Exercises 練習

1 Vocabulary 詞彙

1.1 Common Misspellings 常見拼寫錯誤

請正確拼寫單詞並定義。

1. thret ____________ ______________________________
2. edjucate ____________ ______________________________
3. religis ____________ ______________________________
4. neiborhood ____________ ______________________________
5. scool ____________ ______________________________
6. boycot ____________ ______________________________
7. vilence ____________ ______________________________
8. restrant ____________ ______________________________
9. arest ____________ ______________________________
10. segrigashun ____________ ______________________________

1.2 Homophones 同音異義詞

請寫出一個同音異義詞，並定義兩個單詞。

1. rite ____________ ______________________________

____

2. their ____________ ______________________________

____

3. mourning ____________ ______________________________

____

4. know ____________ ______________________________

____

1.3 Place Names 地名

請將地名與相應的描述連線。

1. A place in Alabama where King was jailed	A. Washington, D.C.
2. A city in Georgia where King was born	B. Montgomery
3. The capitol of the United States where King led a famous march	C. Atlanta
4. A city in Massachusetts where King attended school on a scholarship	D. Birmingham
5. The city where the march from Selma, Alabama ended	E. Boston

1.4 Word Scramble 單詞拼字

請參考定義，整理字母順序使單詞成為書中地名。

1. A city in a state with the same name–**ewn kyor ctiy** ____________
2. The state where King got his Divinity degree–**lavapenynsni** ____________
3. Californian city where King gave a speech–**ols glanees** ____________
4. A place in Illinois that King visited–**agocahic** ____________
5. A location in Texas where President Kennedy was assassinated–**lladas** ____________
6. A town in Alabama where Corretta Scott and King were married–**oinmar** ____________
7. Hartford, a town visited by King, is located in this state–**cutctiencon** ____________

8. A Tennessee city were sanitation workers went on strike–**phsimem** ____________________
9. A city in Michigan where King spoke to thousands–**roittde** ____________________
10. The city in Alabama where a famous march began–**lames** ____________________

Part 2

ROSA PARKS
羅莎・帕克斯

Away from home 離家求學

Rosa Parks, an African American seamstress[1], spent a hard day at her job in Montgomery, Alabama. It was almost Christmas. She had done some shopping. She headed for the bus. She was looking forward to sitting down.

But, as soon as Parks sat down, the bus driver told her to get up. He told her to give her seat to a white man.

It was the 1950s in America. Black people had to sit in the back seats of the bus. But, if a white person was standing,

1 seamstress, *n*: 女裁縫

they were expected to give up those seats to the white person. Rosa Parks refused to get up. She was tired of being mistreated[1] and humiliated[2] just because of the color of her skin.

Park's refusal caused a major court battle[3]. In the end, racial segregation on the buses was declared unconstitutional[4]. Because of what the quiet seamstress had done, black Americans all over the South took a major step toward equality.

Rosa Parks' courage helped launch the civil rights revolution.

Rosa Louise McCauley was born on February 4, 1913, in Tuskegee, Alabama. Her mother, Leona, was a teacher. Her father, James, was a carpenter. Leona McCauley worked hard, cooking and cleaning. James McCauley traveled all around the state doing carpentry work.

---

1 be mistreated, (passive) *v*: 被苛待

2 be humiliated, (passive) *v*: 被羞辱

3 court battle: 官司

4 unconstitutional, *adj*: 違憲

When Leona McCauley was expecting her second child, she moved in with her husband's parents. The house was crowded. Leona was very unhappy.

One day, she packed up baby Rosa. She moved back to her own parents' house in Pine Level, Alabama. Rosa did not see her father again very much. She saw him once when she was a toddler[1]. She saw him again as an adult.

Rosa's brother, Sylvester, was born at their grandparents' house. Rosa liked it there. She loved her grandparents.

When Rosa was about six-years-old, something frightening happened. Her grandfather was sitting by the front door with a shotgun[2] across his knees. He told Rosa that the Ku Klux Klan* was in the neighbourhood. The Ku Klux Klan is a terrorist[3] organization that attacks African Americans.

*Cultural Note

Ku Klux Klan：三K黨，通常也縮寫為KKK。美國歷史上極右翼的民間組織，也是美國種族主義組織的代表。組織認為白人是最優越的種族，歧視其他種族，並施以暴力。

1 toddler, *n*: 學步的孩子

2 shotgun, *n*: 獵槍

3 terrorist, *n*: 恐怖分子

Rosa's grandfather said he would be ready if they tried to break in and harm his family. The Ku Klux Klan did not break in. But, Rosa felt sad that there were white people who would try to harm black people.

Rosa learned an important lesson from her grandfather. You have to stand up for your family and for your principles. When Rosa was older, she got a job picking cotton for fifty cents a day. Many black children in the area worked picking cotton.

Rosa worked from early morning to sundown. It was very hot, and the sun burned down on the children.

As she walked up and down the rows of cotton, she got big, red blisters[1] on her feet. Since the blisters hurt so much, she moved up and down the rows of cotton on her knees[2]. The children had to be

---

1 blister, *n*: 水泡

2 on her knees: 跪着

very careful that they did not get blood from their blisters on the cotton.

At age nine, Rosa started school. There was a nice school for white children and a rundown[1] school for black children. In Rosa's classroom, sixty children were crowded together. But even though it was difficult, Rosa liked to read stories and play games with the other children.

When Rosa was eleven, she went into a store for a soda. The clerk[2] said black children could not sit at the counter and drink sodas. They could have ice cream cones[3] instead. They had to eat them outside the store.

Rosa's mother had a great love for learning. She wanted Rosa to go to a good school. So, Rosa was sent away from her grandparents' farm to the big city of Montgomery, Alabama.

---

1 rundown, *adj*: 破敗

2 clerk, *n:* 店員

3 ice cream cone: 雪糕筒

Found the other half 邂逅另一半

Rosa Parks was enrolled at Montgomery Industrial School for girls. To help pay her tuition[1], Rosa cleaned two classrooms every day.

The school was in Centennial Hill in Montgomery. Like all public and private schools at the time, it was segregated[2] by race. All the students were black but the teachers were white.

The school was started in 1866 by Miss Alice L. White. Miss White was a

---

1 tuition, *n*: 學費

2 be segregated, (passive) *v*: 隔離

Northern white woman who wanted to help the black people get educated after the Civil War.*

Miss White was very strict, but she loved her students. They loved her back because they could see she wanted a better life for them.

Rosa learned a lot from Miss White. She learned a sense of pride. Rosa was a good student. She obeyed her teachers like she obeyed her mother at home.

It was exciting for eleven-year-old Rosa to live in a big city like Montgomery. For the first time in her life, Rosa heard African Americans criticizing[1] segregation.

Rosa thought there was no way to stop segregation. But, she heard an exciting story of how some black people tried to end segregation twenty years earlier.

*Cultural Note

Civil War：美國內戰(1861-1865)，交戰雙方為北方的美利堅合衆國（簡稱聯邦），和南方的美利堅聯盟國（簡稱邦聯）。南方主張保留奴隸制，北方主張廢除奴隸制。最終北方獲得勝利，並廢除奴隸制。

1 criticize, *v*: 批判

In 1900, some black leaders in Montgomery were very upset about how black tram[1] riders were forced to sit in the back of the trams. So, they told black riders to stop using them.

The African Americans in Montgomery did not use the trams for five weeks. They white owners said they could sit anywhere they wanted if they would only come back. The tram owners were losing money.

So, for a little while, tram segregation ended in Montgomery. But then, the white people brought it back. The black riders had to sit in the back again. This story made young Rosa think for the first time that maybe segregation would end one day.

Rosa Parks dreamed of being a teacher like her mother had been. But, when she was sixteen, she learned that her

---

1 tram, *n*: 電車，美 trolley

grandmother was very sick. So, she hurried back to Pine Level to help.

Then, Rosa's mother got sick. Rosa cared for her, too. The family needed money. Rosa returned to Montgomery and worked as a housekeeper[1]. She was eighteen. It seemed her dream of becoming a teacher would not come true.

Rosa McCauley met a young man in Montgomery, Raymond Parks. Like Rosa, he was very religious[2]. He was a member of Rosa's church.

Raymond Parks asked Rosa on a date. She agreed, mostly because he had a shiny, red car. But slowly, Rosa grew to admire Raymond. He did a lot of reading. She loved to talk to him. Raymond Parks was working on an important civil rights case.

---

1 housekeeper, *n*: 管家

2 religious, *adj*: 虔誠

A group of young black men were accused of[1] a terrible crime in Scottsboro, Alabama. They were called the Scottsboro Boys. They were charged with attacking two white women.

The boys ranged in age from twelve to mid-twenties. They denied the charges. But, at the time in the South, the words of blacks did not count for much in court. The boys were convicted[2]. All but the twelve-year-old were sentenced to death. The trial lasted only three days.

Raymond Parks and many other black people believed an injustice[3] was being done to these boys. Parks held meetings and raised money to get the boys a new trial. Rosa McCauley admired his dedication[4] to the cause.

It was dangerous for Parks to try to help the Scottsboro Boys. He could

---

1 be accused of, (passive) *v*: 被指控

2 be convicted, (passive) *v*: 被定罪

3 injustice, *n*: 不公正

4 dedication, *n*: 致力

have been beaten or killed by angry white people. Rosa could see this man had a lot of courage.

Raymond Parks asked Rosa McCauley to marry him. She accepted his proposal. In 1932 they were married. Rosa was nineteen-years-old, and Raymond was twenty-nine. Raymond Parks was a hard-working barber, as well as a civil rights crusader[1].

---

1 crusader, *n*: 改革者

Back to Alabama 情繫故鄉

Raymond Parks and the other civil rights workers had a victory in the case of the Scottsboro Boys*. The United States Supreme Court overturned the convictions[1]. The Court said the young men did not have a fair trial.

Rosa and Raymond Parks did not have money for a honeymoon after their marriage. They moved into a lodging house[2].

Both members of the newly married couple continued to work. Rosa Parks

*Cultural Note

Scottsboro Boys：斯科茨伯勒男孩。1931 年 3 月，9 名黑人男孩被阿拉巴馬州指控，在斯科茨伯勒強姦兩名搭乘同一輛火車的白人女孩。

1 overturn the convictions: 推翻定罪

2 lodging house: 分房出租的公寓，美 rooming house

also helped her husband assemble[1] paperwork on the Scottsboro Boys case. Rosa Parks became more and more involved in the struggle for civil rights for black Americans.

One of the women who had accused the Scottsboro Boys now admitted it was a lie. Even so, the boys were tried again. They were again convicted and sentenced to death.

But, the Supreme Court overturned the second verdict[2] too. The verdict was overturned because there were no African Americans on the jury[3].

Finally, a compromise was reached. The four youngest Scottsboro Boys were freed. The others were paroled[4] after a year. One man, however, was in prison until 1950. Rosa and Raymond Parks had helped save the lives of innocent young men.

---

1 assemble, *v*: 收集

2 verdict, *n*: 裁定

3 on the jury: 陪審

4 be paroled, (passive) *v*: 獲假釋

In 1932 Rosa Parks finally got her high school diploma. She worked as a nurse's assistant. She also sewed clothing for white women.

In 1941 she got a job as a secretary at Russell Field Flight School. This was a federal facility[1], so there was no segregation*. Black and white employees worked and ate together.

Rosa Parks loved the freedom of being treated like everybody else. On buses that rode around the base, she could sit in any seat. But, when she left the federal land and boarded a Montgomery city bus, it was different. She had to sit in the back with the other black people.

Rosa's younger brother, Sylvester McCauley, was drafted[2] in the United States Army. He was to help fight World War II. The military was segregated, so he served in an all black unit.

*Cultural Note

segregation：種族隔離。1877 年，內戰勝利者聯邦政府撤出南方，南方各州建立起種族隔離制度。1896 年聯邦最高法院通過"普萊西訴弗格森案"確認該政策合法，黑人在餐館、商店、學校等公共場所均與白人隔離。

1 federal facility: 聯邦設施

2 be drafted, (passive) *v*: 被徵召

Rosa Parks' interest in civil rights was growing. She joined the National Association for the Advancement of Colored People (NAACP)*. She volunteered to work as a secretary for the local chapter[1]. She wrote letters, arranged meetings, and took care of the office. She was very efficient[2].

In 1945 American soldiers began to return home from the War. Among them were the million black men who had served.

Sylvester McCauley had a fine war record. He helped carry many wounded comrades[3] to safety in bloody battles. McCauley thought that when he got home to Montgomery he would be respected for his service to his country. But, returning black soldiers were mocked[4] and sometimes attacked.

*Cultural Note

NAACP：National Association for the Advancement of Colored People 全國有色人種協進會，始於1909年，是美國的非裔美國人民權組織，成立目的是保證每個人的政治、社會、教育和經濟權利，並消除種族之間的仇恨和歧視。

1 chapter, *n*: 地方分會

2 efficient, *adj*: 高效

3 comrade, *n*: 戰友

4 be mocked, (passive) *v*: 被嘲笑

There were white people who wanted segregation to continue. They were afraid the returning black soldiers would demand equality. So, these white people treated the black veterans[1] even worse than before the war.

McCauley was spat on[2] by some white people in Montgomery. He could not find work. So, he took his wife and two children and moved out of the South. He went to Detroit, Michigan.

Things were not perfect for black people in Detroit, but there was no segregation. McCauley got a good job with the Chrysler Corporation.

Rosa Parks visited her brother in Detroit. She liked the sight of black and white people living together. But, she was homesick for Alabama. She returned to Montgomery. She decided

---

1 veteran, *n*: 老兵

2 be spat on: 受輕視

she would work even harder with the NAACP to make Montgomery a fairer place for blacks.

Rosa Parks was invited to speak at a NAACP convention[1]. She was nervous because she had not done that before. But, she did a good job. She became self-assured[2].

Rosa Parks got a job at Crittenden's Tailor Shop in Montgomery. She was an excellent seamstress. She altered[3] men's suits. She made dresses. Parks also continued to work for the NAACP. She also taught Sunday school. Life was comfortable for them.

---

1 convention, *n*: 會議

2 self-assured, *adj*: 有自信

3 alter, *v*: 改

Started a change 變革開始

On the city buses of Montgomery, Alabama, black riders always had to sit in the back of the bus.

Also, black riders were not treated with courtesy[1]. Drivers often called adult African American women "girl" and adult men "boy." They did not treat them with the respect they showed other riders. Rosa Parks discussed this humiliating[2] situation with her friends at the NAACP.

1 treat with courtesy: 以禮相待

2 humiliating, *adj*: 傷自尊

Seventy-five percent of the people riding the Montgomery bus system were black. Most whites had their own cars. So, the black riders were supporting the bus system. Yet, they were badly treated.

Parks wanted to do something about this. But, she was not sure what she could do. She did not know anything about organizing protests or boycotts.

Some friends of Rosa Parks paid for her to go to a workshop[1] at Highlander Folk School. The school was in the Appalachian Mountains in Tennessee. There she could learn about working for change in society.

When Rosa Parks arrived at Highlander School, she was nervous. Most of the other people were white. Parks felt strange. But, soon she fit in[2] very well.

---

1 workshop, *n*: 研討會

2 fit in: 融入群體

The white people asked her about segregation in Alabama. They were very interested in the stories she told about her experience with the NAACP.

At Highlander School, something happened to Rosa Parks that had never happened before. She was eating food other people made. She had breakfast brought to her on a tray[1]. Parks was forty-two-years-old. It was the first time anybody had waited on[2] her.

After the workshop at Highlander School, Parks returned to Montgomery and her seamstress job. Raymond Parks was now in ill health. He could only work part time. That made it harder on Rosa.

In August 1955 Rosa Parks attended a NAACP meeting. There, she met Rev. Martin Luther King Jr.* for the first time.

*Cultural Note

Rev. Martin Luther King Jr.：馬丁・路德・金，美國牧師，美國民權運動領袖。1955年羅莎・帕克斯因拒向白人讓座被捕，馬丁・路德・金發起蒙哥馬利黑人罷乘運動，最終使聯邦地區法庭裁定阿拉巴馬州巴士實行種族隔離的法律違憲。

1 tray, *n*: 托盤

2 wait on sb: 服侍某人

She was very inspired by[1] him. He seemed strong and fearless. Rosa Parks had fresh hope that conditions might indeed change for black people in the American South.

During the summer of 1955, Rosa Parks continued to work hard and volunteer at the NAACP. She did not expect anything dramatic to happen to her. But, her life and the whole system of segregation was about to be shaken.

On a rainy evening on December 1, 1955, Rosa Parks left her seamstress job as usual. She headed home. She ached[2] all over from the long hours she spent hunched over her work[3]. Rosa Parks had bursitis[4], a problem that causes pain in the joints.

The first bus that came was too crowded. Parks did not want to stand on

---

1 be inspired by, (passive) *v*: 受鼓舞

2 ache, *v*: 疼痛

3 hunched over one's work: 俯身工作

4 bursitis, *n*: 滑囊炎

the ride home. So, while waiting for the next bus, she did some Christmas shopping.

When Parks returned to the bus stop, she put her money in the fare box. Then, she went down the aisle[1] to a seat. All of the front seats were for white riders. The back seats were for black riders. But the seats in the middle were for anybody on a first come, first served[2] basis.

Parks sat down in the middle section next to a black man. She was glad to be off her feet[3] and heading home at last.

When the bus stopped at the next corner, some white passengers boarded. The entire front section for whites only filled up rapidly. Some of the white riders were standing.

---

1 aisle, *n*: 通道

2 first come, first served: 先到先得

3 off one's feet: 坐着

The bus driver came down the middle aisle. The rule was that no white rider would have to stand, even if that meant that black people would have to give up their seats. The bus driver came to the row of seats where Rosa Parks was sitting.

There were four African Americans in that row: Parks, a black man, and two black women across the aisle.

The bus driver told them all to get up so that the white man could take one of the seats. It was not allowed for a white person to sit in a row also occupied[1] by black people. Once the white man sat down, the entire row became a "white row."

The black man and the two black women got up as they were told to do. Rosa Parks refused to move.

---

1 occupy, *v*: 佔用

First victory 首戰告捷

The bus driver told Rosa Parks to get up or he would have her arrested. She refused. The bus sat there until two white police officers arrived. The officers arrested Rosa Parks and took her to jail.

Parks was led up a narrow flight of stairs to her cell. It smelled bad in the jail. Everything was dirty. Parks was put in a cell with other women.

Rosa Parks was arrested and fingerprinted.
羅莎・帕克斯被捕並被採集指紋。

Parks asked if she could make a phone call. She wanted to tell her husband what had happened. He was expecting her home. The jailer refused to let her make a phone call until an hour had passed. Then, finally, Rosa Parks called and told her husband she was in jail.

Word had already spread through the black community that Rosa Parks had been arrested. People who knew her saw the police taking her off the bus. Now, Raymond Parks and some white and black friends came to the jail. They paid Rosa Parks' bail[1] and took her home.

Soon there was a meeting of the NAACP. The leaders saw the arrest of Rosa Parks as a chance to end bus segregation in Montgomery and the entire nation.

First, the black people of Montgomery would boycott[2] the bus system. Rosa Parks would then be convicted of breaking the segregation law. At that point, the NAACP would appeal[3].

They would take the case all the way to the United States Supreme Court. They were hoping the Court would declare segregation on public transportation unconstitutional.

Rosa Parks' elderly mother lived with her. Raymond Parks was not well. Rosa Parks supported her family. She was

---

1 bail, *n*: 保釋金

2 boycott, *v*: 聯合抵制

3 appeal, *v*: 上訴

afraid she might be fired from her job. But even though she was worried, she agreed to help with the bus boycott.

To start the bus boycott, the black leaders in Montgomery turned to two young ministers. They were Reverend Ralph Abernathy and Reverend Martin Luther King Jr. There were meetings in the black churches of Montgomery to plan the boycott.

The bus boycott was set for December 5, 1955. No black man, woman, or child was to ride the buses that day.

Thousands of leaflets[1] were printed and given throughout the black neighborhoods. People were told to find other ways to get to school or work. If they had to, they were told to walk wherever they had to go.

The weather was cold on the morning of December 5. Rosa Parks and the

---

1 leaflet, *n*: 傳單

other black supporters of the boycott were fearful. They thought most black people would want to ride the buses.

Many had long trips to work. They had no way to ride to work in automobiles. Most blacks had no automobiles and did not know anyone who did. It would be a terrible hardship to walk for many miles and then put in a hard day's work.

But, on that Monday morning, the black people of Montgomery surprised everyone. They boycotted the buses. The buses were empty as they rolled through the streets. The boycott was a big success.

The leaders of the boycott were from the Montgomery Improvement Association (MIA)*. They decided to keep the boycott going until the city of Montgomery gave in to their demands.

*Cultural Note

Montgomery Improvement Association (MIA)：蒙哥馬利改進協會。成立於1955年，組織領袖為馬丁・路德・金。該組織在蒙哥馬利巴士聯合抵制運動中發揮了重要作用。

The MIA demanded fair and courteous[1] treatment for black riders. They also demanded black bus drivers on black routes. They insisted that seats should be given out on a first come, first served basis. Black people should not be expected to give up seats they already had to white newcomers.

The MIA made plans to help the boycotting riders. They set up fleets[2] of taxicabs, which charged the same fare as the bus. The few black people who did own automobiles agreed to carpool[3]. Many adults and children promised to keep on walking for as long as necessary.

Rosa Parks came to court and was convicted of breaking the bus segregation law. She was fined ten dollars. Rosa Parks appealed the sentence. The whole issue of bus segregation was now on its way to the U.S. Supreme Court.

---

1 courteous, *adj*: 禮貌

2 fleet, *n*: 車隊

3 carpool, *v*: 共乘

Headed for Michigan 轉戰密歇根

In January 1956 Rosa Parks lost her job. She was fired. She did not think it was because of the bus boycott. But, it was very hard for the family.

Parks took part time sewing jobs to keep food on the table. Parks spent a lot of time doing volunteer work for the MIA. She found ways for many black people to get to work without using the bus. She coordinated rides for people. She helped set up special bus stops for black taxicabs at black churches.

As the boycott continued, the white business community was suffering. Black people did not shop in downtown Montgomery anymore.

The bus companies were desperate with all of their black riders gone. Some white people became angry. They made threats against Rosa and others.

On January 30, somebody planted[1] a bomb at Rev. Martin Luther King's house. His wife and baby were inside the house. If they had not been in the back of the house, they might have been hurt or killed.

Some white people blamed King for making the bus boycott more effective. In February, Parks, King, and 86 other civil rights activists were arrested for setting up the bus boycott. There was an Alabama state law against boycotts.

---

1 plant, *v*: 放置

Rosa Parks was becoming world famous now. News reporters came from all over the world to see what was happening in Montgomery. It was all because Rosa Parks refused to give up her seat to a white man on that bus.

Many people praised Parks for her courage. But, life was very hard for Parks and her family. Leona McCauley, Rosa's mother, was very ill. Raymond Parks was nervous and sick. He could not work.

All the pressure was having an effect on the family. Rosa Parks had no steady job. She found it hard to pay her bills. For the first time in her life, Parks took money from her friends to keep going.

On June 5, 1956, the federal court ruled that Alabama's bus segregation law was unconstitutional. They said it violated[1] the Fourteenth Amendment*, which gave equal protection to all Americans.

Alabama appealed to the United States Supreme Court. In November the Supreme Court agreed that bus segregation was unconstitutional. That meant all buses all over the South had to be integrated[2]. Black people could no longer be told they had to sit in certain seats.

The bus boycott was over. The civil rights workers had won. Rosa Parks had won.

In December Rosa Parks got on a Montgomery city bus. She sat where she wanted. Nobody said a word.

The integration of Montgomery's bus system went well overall. But, there were some ugly incidents. Somebody fired a

*Cultural Note

Fourteenth Amendment：美國憲法第十四條修正案，於1868年通過，內容規定所有公民享有平等的受保護權。修正案還包括國籍、眾議員選舉等其他內容。

1 violate, *v*: 違背

2 be integrated, (passive) *v*: 被取消種族隔離

Rosa Parks seated on a Montgomery City bus.
羅莎・帕克斯乘坐蒙哥馬利市的巴士。

shotgun blast at Rev. Martin Luther King Jr.'s front door. Fortunately, nobody was hurt.

A sniper[1] shot a black bus rider in the leg. Several black churches were bombed. But, nobody was hurt. Little by little, the white people of Montgomery accepted what had happened. All charges against Rosa Parks and her friends were dropped.

Rosa Parks had helped win a great victory for the black people of the

1 sniper, *n*: 狙擊手

American South. But, she continued to get threats. People called her home and warned her to get out of Montgomery. Parks loved Montgomery. She did not want to leave.

Parks' husband was so upset. He seemed to have a nervous breakdown[1]. Parks' mother was suffering too. Rosa Parks decided she could no longer ask her family to pay such a high price.

The Parks family was also suffering financially. Rosa Parks could not get a job anymore. Everybody knew who she was. White employers feared trouble if they hired her. There were very few black employers in Montgomery.

Rosa Parks sadly packed up her few possessions. They headed to the only place where they had family, Detroit, Michigan.

1 nervous breakdown: 神經衰竭

Remained humble 淡泊名利

Sylvester McCauley, Rosa Parks' brother, owned a large house in Detroit*. He and his wife, Daisy, had thirteen children. When Rosa Parks arrived in Detroit, her brother helped her get settled. Rosa Parks joined the local NAACP. She looked for work.

Rosa Parks was offered a job in Virginia. She hoped to work in Detroit, but she needed to bring in money. So, she left her husband and mother in

*Cultural Note

Detroit: 底特律市，美國密歇根州最大的城市。城市通過底特律河連接五大湖，即北美洲重要的湖泊。汽車產業發達，有"汽車城"的美譽。

Detroit. She worked for the Hampton Institute in Virginia as a hostess[1] in the guest residence.

Parks worked at the Hampton Institute for a year. Then, she came back to Detroit and got a job at a small shop as a seamstress. She worked ten hours a day at the sewing machine making aprons[2] and skirts. It was hard work, but now Parks could support her family.

While working at the shop, Parks met a black teenager, Elaine Eason. The young woman was impressed with Rosa Parks. She had read about her in the newspapers. She could not believe Parks was a seamstress in Detroit.

Elaine Eason asked Rosa Parks all about the Montgomery bus boycott and what it was like. Eason felt like she was

---

1 hostess, *n*: 女招待

2 apron, *n*: 圍裙

talking to a celebrity. From then on, Rosa Parks and Elaine Eason (who became Elaine Eason Steele) were good friends.

Parks continued to be involved in civil rights activities. In August 1963 Rev. Martin Luther King Jr. led a large march for justice on Washington, D.C. Parks was there.

Then, in early 1964, Rosa Parks heard about a young black man trying to get elected to the House of Representatives from Michigan. Thirty-five-year-old John Conyers, Jr. was a lawyer. He was also a hardworking friend of civil rights causes. But, Conyers was not well-known. He would have a difficult time getting elected.

Rosa Parks thought John Conyers Jr. was just what the people needed in that district. She decided to help him get elected. She called Martin Luther King Jr. and asked him to come to Michigan to speak for Conyers.

King never made political speeches for people. But, he was convinced[1] by Parks that he should make this speech. He came to Michigan and asked voters to elect Conyers. It was just what the Conyers' campaign needed. John Conyers, Jr. won the election.

When he joined the House of Representatives, John Conyers asked Rosa Parks to join the staff in his Michigan office. Some of Conyers' friends thought this was not a good idea. Parks was controversial[2]. She had been in the middle of that bus boycott in Alabama.

But, Parks took the job and turned out to be an excellent congressional[3]

---

1 be convinced, (passive) *v*: 被說服

2 controversial, *adj*: 有爭議

3 congressional, *adj*: 國會

assistant. When people brought problems to Congressman[1] Conyers' office, Rosa Parks handled them. She brought important issues to Conyers' attention. Parks was courteous and efficient.

Some white people in Michigan knew about Rosa Parks' past in ending bus segregation in Alabama. Some of them sent her hate mail. The letters ridiculed[2] Parks. But, none of this bothered Rosa Parks. She had been through too much already to let hate mail get her down.

Rosa Parks became a member of St. Matthews American Methodist Episcopalian (AME) church in Detroit. She was made a deaconess[3].

In her job, she reached out to the sick and needy[4] of the church and tried to help them. She visited church members

---

1 congressman, *n*: 國會議員

2 ridicule, *v*: 嘲弄

3 deaconess, *n*: 教會女執事

4 needy, *n*: 窮人

in nursing homes[1] and hospitals and prison.

Sometimes people would come to the church just to see her rushing around doing her work. They remembered seeing her picture in all the papers during the Montgomery bus boycott. Now here she was, quietly working in her church to help the needy.

Rosa Parks never took credit for having done anything outstanding. She just did what had to be done and remained a humble[2] person. She knew she was well known because of the Montgomery bus boycott. But, she did not care about that.

---

1 nursing home: 私立療養院

2 humble, *adj*: 謙遜

Lost her loved ones 痛失親友

In March 1965 a group of African Americans marched from Selma to Montgomery, Alabama. Black people were being denied the right to vote in some places in the South. The marchers called attention to this.

Rosa Parks was watching the march on television from her home in Detroit. Suddenly, something terrible happened. White Alabama state troopers[1] attacked the marchers with clubs[2]. Men and women were knocked to the ground.

---

1 trooper, *n*: 州警察

2 club, *n*: 棍

The marchers ran to a church and hoped they would be safe there. But, the troopers followed them into the church. They threw one man right through a stained glass[1] window.

Rosa Parks was horrified. She had taken part in demonstrations. But, nobody had ever treated her like these marchers were treated.

Martin Luther King Jr. called Parks and asked her to come to Alabama. He wanted her to join him in another march. Parks had no money for the plane ticket. But, her brother's trade union paid for her ticket. She was off to Alabama.

King led the march this time. The Alabama state troopers watched. But, this time they did not attack the marchers. Rosa Parks was happy to have taken part in this march.

---

1 stained glass: 彩色玻璃

In 1967 there were race riots[1] in Detroit. Rosa Parks spoke out against the violence. She understood that the young men were frustrated and angry. But, what they had done did not help themselves or others. They burned businesses. Rosa Parks' husband was working at a barbershop at the time. He lost all of his tools in the fires.

On the night of April 4, 1968, Rosa Parks and her mother were watching television. A bulletin[2] flashed on the screen. Martin Luther King Jr. had been assassinated[3].

Parks and her mother wept at the news. King had done so much to advance the cause of civil rights. Now, he had been shot down and killed. Rosa Parks was filled with deep sadness.

Rosa Parks was now suffering from health problems. She had stomach

---

1 riot, *n*: 暴亂

2 bulletin, *n*: 簡明新聞

3 be assassinated, (passive) *v*: 遭暗殺

ulcers[1] and heart trouble. In the 1970s, Parks fell down twice, breaking bones. She still worked for Congressman Conyers. She was supporting her mother and, most of the time, her husband too. She had to keep going no matter how she felt.

For five years Raymond Parks suffered from throat cancer. Rosa Parks worried and kept hoping he would recover. She loved and respected her husband.

Raymond Parks was not perfect, but he had many good qualities. He did not mind that Rosa Parks' mother lived with the family. He never complained about having his mother-in-law in the home.

Raymond Parks was often very worried about his wife's participation in civil rights causes. He was so nervous that he sometimes could not sleep at night. But, he knew how much this

---

1 stomach ulcer: 胃潰瘍

work meant to Rosa Parks. He never asked her to give it up.

In 1977 Raymond Parks died. Rosa Parks was grief stricken. All through their marriage, Raymond Parks was often out of work and sick. But, the fact that he was always there giving his wife moral support meant so much to Rosa Parks. Now that he was gone, she mourned[1] for him deeply.

A few months after Raymond Parks died, Rosa Parks suffered another terrible personal blow[2]. Her brother, Sylvester McCauley, also died. When they were children, Rosa Parks always took care of him. Now, he too was gone.

At this time Leona McCauley was also under treatment for cancer. Parks was working full time for Congressman Conyers. It was a very hard time in Rosa Parks' life.

---

1 mourn, *v*: 哀悼

2 blow, *n*: 打擊

The freedom ride 自由之旅

Rosa Parks managed to care for her mother for two years while working full time. In 1979, ninety-one-year-old Leona McCauley died. Rosa Parks was nearing seventy. Now, she was all alone.

In 1979 Rosa Parks was given an award called the Spingarn Medal by the NAACP for her civil rights work. She also won the Martin Luther King Jr. Nonviolent Peace Prize.

She kept on working and overcoming her loneliness. Then, her friendship with Elaine Steel grew more important. The teenager she had met years before at the sewing machines was now like a daughter.

Elaine Steele helped Parks realize she would soon have to retire. Parks needed to develop new interests. At Steele's urging, Parks attended aerobics classes and studied holistic health[1].

The project that was most important to Rosa Parks now was the Rosa and Raymond Parks Institute[2] for Self Development. Students at the Institute were urged[3] to develop to their full potential[4]. A program called Pathways to Freedom took students on tours around the United States.

Rosa Parks and Elaine Steele took a group of students to see the place where

1 holistic health: 整體健康

2 institute, *n*: 學院

3 be urged, (passive) *v*: 被要求

4 potential, *n* : 潛力

the Selma to Montgomery March took place. They also visited sites along the Underground Railroad*. These sites were safe houses where fleeing[1] slaves hid out[2]. During the times of slavery[3], they hid while on their way to freedom in Canada.

Parks wanted these young people to know their heritage[4]. She wanted them to understand the sacrifices black people made before them. These sacrifices were made so that they could have more equality in their lives.

Thousands of young people from all over the United States took these Pathways to Freedom tours in the 1980s.

In 1988 at age seventy-four, Rosa Parks retired from Congressman Conyers' office. Her eyesight was poor. She was growing very tired. She knew

*Cultural Note

Underground Railroad ：秘密路線，美國 19 世紀黑人奴隸逃離至美國北方和加拿大，逃離途中所使用的線路和安全住處構成的網路就是秘密路線。

1 fleeing, *adj*: 逃跑
2 hide out: 躲藏
3 slavery, *n*: 奴隸制
4 heritage, *n*: 傳統

she could no longer give her job the energy it deserved.

Rosa Parks never did anything half way. She needed to give her all. But, her age was now catching up with her.

Rosa Parks was always interested in young people. She believed the job of the adult world was to show young people the way and to inspire them. She wanted to make the world a better place for the next generation.

To reach out to young people, Rosa Parks became an author. She wrote several books. The first book was titled *My Story*. It told how Rosa Parks refused to give up her seat on that bus. It was about how this led to the bus boycott and the end of bus segregation. She wrote in her own simple, direct way.

Rosa Parks wrote the book *Quiet Strength* to share her philosophy of life with youth. The book talked about the things that were very important to Parks. She wrote of her own religious faith and the values she held dear. She also wrote about the need to be determined to do your best.

For many years, children and young people wrote letters to Rosa Parks. Sometimes they were having problems in their own lives. They wanted her advice. Sometimes they were just curious about how Rosa Parks felt when she was sent to jail.

Parks gathered many of these letters. From them, she wrote her third book, *Dear Mrs. Parks.* She included the letters of the young people and her answers to them.

One young writer wanted to know why racism[1] still continued to exist in the

---

1 racism, *n*: 種族主義

world. He could not understand why some people disliked others just because their skin was a different color.

Rosa Parks told the boy that everybody has to work together for a better world. She said that God created all people no matter what color they were.

For the first time in Rosa Parks' life, she had enough money to be comfortable. She had always struggled to make ends meet.

The royalties[1] from her books, although not great, were enough to pay her bills. She even had a little left over. Rosa Parks was surprised to find that she had enough money that she did not have to worry anymore.

---

1 royalties, [pl], *n*: 版稅

Rosa Parks never took a trip outside the United States until she was eighty years old. Then, she was invited to go to Japan and speak to the young people there. Rosa Parks was wondering if the youth of Japan really knew who she was.

When she arrived in Japan she was amazed to see eight thousand Japanese children lining the streets to greet her. They all were singing "We Shall Overcome," the famous civil rights hymn used in many of the marches.

When Parks returned to the United States, she spoke at schools all over the country. She enjoyed talking to children and hearing their hopes and dreams for the future. Rosa Parks lived in a Detroit apartment alone. One night a terrible thing happened.

She was getting ready for bed when a young black man broke into the apartment. The man asked Parks for money. She went to her purse to get him some money. Then, he began to hit her. He punched[1] her in the face many times.

Parks tried to fight the man off. Finally, he knocked her down and took all of her money, about one hundred dollars.

Rosa Parks called Elaine Steele for help. She lived close by. She came over quickly. The police came and Parks was taken to the hospital. Luckily, she was not badly hurt. She said she did not hate the young man who had attacked her. She could not hate anybody.

After the attack, Rosa Parks moved to a more secure apartment. But, she did not go into seclusion[2]. She kept on visiting schools and talking to young people. In one school in Philadelphia,

---

1 punch, *v*: 猛擊

2 seclusion, *n*: 隱居

the children chanted her name as she drove up. The children listened attentively[1] to what she had to say.

In 1996 President Bill Clinton gave Rosa Parks the Medal of Freedom. In 1999 she received the Congressional Gold Medal.

President Clinton told the audience that when he was a little boy he had read in the newspaper about this brave woman. She was the woman who refused to give up her seat on a bus in Montgomery, Alabama. He said he was inspired by Rosa Parks' courage when he was a boy. Now, he was proud to honour[2] her.

In December 2000 the Rosa Parks Library and Museum opened at Troy State University in Montgomery, Alabama. The museum is on the exact

---

1 attentively, *adv*: 專注

2 honour, *v*: 給…以榮譽，[美] honor

spot[1] where Rosa Parks was arrested that day in 1955.

In 2002 a movie was made about Rosa Parks. It was called *Ride to Freedom: The Rosa Parks Story.*

The Rosa Parks Library and Museum in Montgomery, Alabama.
位於阿拉巴馬州蒙哥馬利的羅莎・帕克斯圖書館暨博物館。

---

1 spot, *n*: 地點

A fairer world 社會更公平

Rosa Parks was confined to[1] a wheelchair in her later years. But, she continued to speak out on civil rights issues. She was an ordinary woman, a seamstress who never thought she would become famous.

Her act of courage and dignity[2] that day in Montgomery changed history. For decades, black men and women had been forced to sit in the backs of the buses. They had to accept rudeness and humiliation throughout the South.

---

1 be confined to, (passive) *v*: 受局限

2 dignity, *n*: 尊嚴

But one quiet, gentle woman took a chance. She risked her safety and her livelihood[1]. For that, equality was advanced.

Rosa Parks died in 2005 at the age of ninety-two. She was a nonviolent revolutionary who made the United States a more just society. She did not do it for money or for fame[2]. Neither of these had much meaning to her. She did it for the simple reason that it was the right thing to do. She did it to make the world a better place.

---

1 livelihood, *n*: 生計

2 fame, *n*: 名望

Exercises 練習

1 Vocabulary 詞彙

1.1 Synonyms and antonyms 同反義詞

請分別以 A/S 標示反義詞、同義詞。

____ 1. peace—war	____ 7. short—long
____ 2. difficult—simple	____ 8. struggle—fight
____ 3. accuse—blame	____ 9. public—private
____ 4. celebrate—mourn	____ 10. near—close
____ 5. separate—segregate	____ 11. just—fair
____ 6. brave—cowardly	____ 12. victory—defeat

1.2 Synonyms and antonyms 同反義詞

請各寫一個同義詞、反義詞。

同義詞		反義詞
1. ____________	non-violent	____________
2. ____________	humble	____________
3. ____________	unconstitutional	____________
4. ____________	controversial	____________
5. ____________	injustice	____________

1.3 Specialized vocabulary 專業詞彙

寫出單詞短語的定義，生詞請查閱字典。多義詞請寫出與平等權利運動相關的定義。

1. segregation ____________________
2. prejudice ____________________
3. demonstration ____________________
4. sit-in ____________________

5. boycott ______________________________

6. petition ______________________________

7. strike ______________________________

8. protest ______________________________

9. picket line ______________________________

10. march ______________________________

11. discrimination ______________________________

12. appeal ______________________________

13. Act ______________________________

14. unjust ______________________________

2 Initial understanding 初步理解

2.1 Identify structure 標記結構

辨析句子邏輯，在空白處標示相應的單詞簡寫：
MI/SD: 主題和細節，C/E: 因果， SOE: 事件順序，
C/C: 類比和反比。

____ 1. As a child, Rosa Parks enjoyed school. She liked to read and play games with the other children.

____ 2. The Scottsboro boys were charged with attacking two white women. Because they were black, the trial was very short and unjust.

____ 3. In the 1950s, Rosa Parks lived in Montgomery, Alabama, where segregation was everywhere. She saw that Detroit, on the other hand, was more integrated.

____ 4. Rosa Parks worked hard for equal rights. As a boy and an adult, President Bill Clinton came to admire her. He then awarded her the Medal of Freedom in 1996. In 1999 she received the Congressional Gold Medal.

____ 5. Martin Luther King, Jr. was a preacher who was comfortable giving speeches. Rosa Parks was quiet and humble and didn't like public attention.

____ 6. The black people of Montgomery boycotted the city bus system. The boycott was successful, and the Supreme Court ruled that bus segregation was unconstitutional.

____ 7. Rosa Parks became increasingly interested in civil rights. Then, she joined the NAACP. After a while, she was asked to give speeches about civil rights.

____ 8. The bus driver told Rosa to get up, but Rosa refused to give up her seat. She was taken to jail because of this.

____ 9. Rosa Parks was an inspirational leader during the Civil Rights Movement. She courageously refused to give up her seat on the Montgomery bus. She dedicated her life to the fight for equality.

____10. Rosa Parks got onto the bus. She sat down in a seat. Then, the bus driver told her to stand up to make room for a white passenger.

Answer Key 答案

Part 1 Martin Luther King Jr.

1 Vocabulary

1.1 Common Misspellings

1. thret: threat: a warning of possible trouble
2. edjucate: educate: to provide schooling or training
3. religis: religious: having to do with religion or a belief in higher powers
4. neibourhood: neighbourhood: the area around a place
5. scool: school: a place where students are educated
6. boycot: boycott: to stop buying or using
7. vilence: violence: swift and intense force
8. restrant: restaurant: a place for dining
9. arest: arrest: to seize by legal authority
10. segrigashun: segregation: separation due to race or ethnicity

1.2 Homophones

1. rite: a ceremonial act right: a just claim write: to trace on paper
2. their: belonging to them they're: a contraction of "they are" there: in or at that place
3. mourning: the feeling of loss morning: the early part of the day
4. know: to understand as fact or truth no: the opposite of yes; a negative used to express dissent

1.3 Place Names

1. D, 2. C, 3. A, 4. E, 5. B

1.4 Word Scramble

1. New York City
2. Pennsylvania
3. Los Angeles
4. Chicago
5. Dallas
6. Marion
7. Connecticut
8. Memphis
9. Detroit
10. Selma

Part 2 Rosa Parks

1 Vocabulary

1.1 Synonyms and antonyms

1. A 2. A 3. S 4. A 5. S 6. A 7. A 8. S
9. A 10. S 11. S 12. A

1.2 Synonyms and antonyms

1. peaceful [non-violent] aggressive
2. modest [humble] arrogant
3. unlawful [unconstitutional] lawful
4. problematic [controversial] unquestionable
5. inequity [injustice] justice

1.3 Specialized vocabulary

1. **segregation**: the separation of people based on race or ethnicity
2. **prejudice**: unreasonable feelings or opinions regarding race or ethnicity

3. **demonstration**: a public act of protest
4. **sit-in**: an organized passive protest in which people occupy an area and refuse to leave
5. **boycott**: to stop buying or using something in protest
6. **petition**: a formal request containing the signatures of many supporters of the request
7. **strike**: to stop doing something as a coercive act
8. **protest**: an expression of objection
9. **picket line**: a line of strikers
10. **march**: an organized protest walk
11. **discrimination**: treatment against a group based on race or ethnicity
12. **appeal**: an application for review by a higher legal body
13. **Act**: a decree resulting from a decision made by a legislative body
14. **unjust**: unfair

2 Initial understanding

2.1 Identify structure

1. MI/SD
2. C/E
3. C/C
4. SOE
5. C/C
6. C/E
7. SOE
8. C/E
9. MI/SD
10. SOE

English-Chinese Vocabulary List
中英對照生詞表

Proper names
專有名詞

Appalachian Mountains
阿巴拉契亞山脈

Chicagoan 芝加哥人

Chrysler Corporation
佳士拿汽車公司

Civil War
美國內戰

Connecticut 康涅狄格州

Hartford 哈特福德

Ku Klux Klan 美國三 K 黨

Memphis 孟菲斯

Montgomery 蒙哥馬利

Supreme Court 最高法院

The Fourteenth Amendment
第十四條修正案

Tuskegee 塔斯基吉

Vietnamese 越南人

General Vocabulary
一般詞彙

accusation 譴責

ache 疼痛

address 演講

aisle 通道

ally 盟友

alter 改

answer violence with violence 以暴制暴

aorta 主動脈

appeal 上訴

apron 圍裙

arrest 逮捕

artery 動脈

assemble 收集

attentively 專注

autograph 親筆簽名

bail 保釋金

banister 樓梯欄杆

befall 降臨

be accused of 被指控

be appointed 被任命

be assassinated 遭暗殺

be averted 被避免

be confined to 受局限

be confronted by 面對

be convicted 被判有罪

be convinced 被說服

be crushed to death 被壓死

be desegregated
被廢除種族隔離

be drafted 被徵召

be grabbed by the throat
被掐住頸部

be humiliated 被羞辱

be indicted 被起訴

be integrated
被取消種族隔離

be inspired by 受鼓舞

be mistreated 被苛待

be mocked 被嘲笑

be outlawed 被宣告非法

be paroled 獲假釋

be segregated 被隔離

be shoved 被猛推

be spat on 受輕視

be urged 被要求

be yanked 被猛拉

blade 刀刃

blanket 毯子

blight 破壞

blister 水泡

blood vessel 血管

blow 打擊

boycott 聯合抵制

breastbone 胸骨

bulletin 簡明新聞

bursitis 滑囊炎

carpool 共乘

catastrophe 災難

chapter 地方分會

charge 指控

civil rights 公民權

clerk 店員

club 棍

cockroach-infested
蟑螂成群

coffin 靈柩，美 casket

comfort 安慰

commitment 投身

comrade 戰友

congressional 國會

congressman 國會議員

conservatory 音樂學院

controversial 有爭議

convention 會議

conviction 定罪

convince 說服
coordinate 協調
court battle 官司
courteous 禮貌
courthouse 法院大樓
creed 信仰
criticize 批判
crumbling 剝落
crusade 改革運動
crusader 改革者
deaconess 教會女執事
decent 像樣
declare 宣佈
dedication 致力
delivery 演講方式
denied 不被承認
despair 絕望
dignity 尊嚴
dismiss 不理會
disobedient 不服從
Divinity degree 神學學位
dread 懼怕
dreadful 可怕
drifter 流浪漢
dustcart 垃圾車，[美] garbage truck
dynamite sticks 炸藥棒
ease poverty 減少貧困
efficient 高效
eloquently 有說服力
emotional 有感染力
erupt 爆發
ex-convict 前科犯
fame 名望
federal facility 聯邦設施
first come, first served 先到先得
fit in 融入群體
fleeing 逃跑
fleet 車隊
following one's footsteps 步人後塵
funeral parlor 殯儀館
furious 憤怒
gas stove 煤氣爐
get at 足夠取出
glee club 合唱團
handcuff 手銬
harassment 騷擾
heritage 傳統
high pressure hose 高壓水槍
holistic health 整體健康
homemaker 主婦
honour 給…以榮譽，[美] honor
hostess 女招待
housekeeper 管家
humble 謙遜
humiliating 傷自尊
hunched over one's work 俯身工作
ice cream cone 雪糕筒
injustice 不公正
institute 學院
integration 種族融合
interstate 州際
intervene 介入
jaw 下巴
jawbone 下顎骨
juror 陪審員
just 公正
leaflet 傳單
legacy 遺產
legal matter 法律問題
legislation 立法
listening device 竊聽器
livelihood 生計
lodging house 分房出租的公寓，[美] rooming house
massive 大型
mattress 牀墊
minister 牧師
mob 暴民
momentous 重大
monstrous 駭人聽聞
mourn 哀悼
mourning 哀悼
needy 窮人
neighbourhood 社區，[美] neighborhood
nervous breakdown 神經衰竭
newlyweds 新婚夫婦
nursing home 私立療養院
occupy 佔用
off one's feet 坐着
on her knees 跪着
on the jury 陪審
overthrow 推翻
overturn the convictions 推翻定罪
parade 遊行
paramedic 護理人員
parsonage 牧師住宅
pastor 牧師
pastorate 牧師任期
penalty 罰金
perform the ceremony 主持儀式
pew 長椅

plant 埋設
plead 辯護
pledge 承諾
plunge 插入
pocket 小地區
police commissioner 警察局長
porch 門廊
potential 潛力
preach a sermon 佈道
prestige 威望
pull out 退出
pull over 停車
punch 猛擊
racial hatred 種族仇恨
racism 種族主義
railway carriage 火車車廂，美 railroad car
rampant 猖獗
razor-sharp 鋒利
rebellious 叛逆
release 釋放
religious 虔誠
remains 遺骸
resume 重新開始
rib 肋骨
ridicule 嘲弄
rifle 步槍
riot 暴亂
rip out 炸開
royalties 版税
rundown 破敗
scrap 碎片
seamstress 女裁縫
seclusion 隱居
self-assured 有自信
senator 參議員
sermon 講道
shabby 破舊
shack 棚屋
sharecropper 佃農
shotgun 獵槍
sit-in 靜坐抗議
slavery 奴隸制
sniper 狙擊手
sob 哭泣
spinal cord 脊髓
sponsored 資助
spot 地點
spray 飛濺
stab 刺
stained glass 彩色玻璃
stand trial 受審
stand up for 捍衛
stand up to 反抗
stir up 煽動
stomach ulcer 胃潰瘍
storey 樓層，美 story
stride 大步走
survivor benefits 遺屬撫恤金
sweep…into the spotlight 使 … 成為焦點
tax fraud 税務欺詐
tent city 帳篷城
terrorist 恐怖分子
thrilled 興奮
thud 重擊聲
tobacco 煙草
toddler 學步的孩子
traffic violation 交通違規
tram 電車，美 trolley
trample 踩踏
tray 托盤
treat with courtesy 以禮相待
trial 審判
trooper 州警察
tuition 學費
unconstitutional 違憲
undermine 逐漸破壞
unemployment compensation 失業救濟
unrest urge 竭力主張
vandalism 故意破壞
verdict 裁定
veteran 老兵
violate 違背
wages 工資
wait on sb 服侍某人
weary 疲勞
whip 鞭打
workshop 研討會
wrestle 摔跤

Timeline of Martin Luther King Jr.
馬丁·路德·金年表

Events in the life of Martin Luther King Jr.

January 15, 1929	King was born in Atlanta, Georgia. 馬丁・路德・金出生於喬治亞州的亞特蘭大。
1947	King was appointed Assistant Pastor at Ebenezer Church. 馬丁・路德・金被任命埃比尼澤浸信會的牧師助理。
1951	King received his Divinity degree from Crozer Theological Seminar. 馬丁・路德・金獲得柯羅澤神學院的神學學位。
1955	The Montgomery bus boycott was launched. 蒙哥馬利巴士聯合抵制運動發起。
1956	The Kings' house was bombed. The federal court declared the bus segregation was illegal. 馬丁・路德・金家被投擲炸彈。聯邦法庭宣佈巴士種族隔離違法。
1957	The Southern Christian Leadership Conference was founded and King was chosen as president. King received the Spingarn Medal. 南方基督教領袖會議成立，馬丁・路德・金任會長，同年獲得斯平加恩獎章。
1959	King became co-pastor of Ebenezer Baptist Church with his father. 馬丁・路德・金與父親一起成為埃比尼澤浸信會的牧師。
1963	King was arrested in the demonstration in Birmingham and wrote an essay "Letter from a Birmingham jail". 馬丁・路德・金在伯明翰的遊行中被捕，寫下《伯明翰監獄來信》。
August 28, 1963	King made the famous speech "I have a dream". 馬丁・路德・金發表著名演講《我有一個夢想》。
1964	King was awarded the Nobel Peace Prize. 馬丁・路德・金獲得諾貝爾和平獎。

April 4, 1968	King was shot to death by a white man who hated black people. 馬丁・路德・金被一名仇視黑人的白人槍殺。
1969	King's widow began to build The Martin Luther King Jr. Center for Nonviolent Social Change. 馬丁・路德・金的遺孀開始修建“非暴力社會變革——馬丁・路德・金中心”。
1982	The center was opened and King's body was brought there. 中心對外開放，馬丁・路德・金的遺體被移入。

Timeline of Rosa Parks
羅莎・帕克斯年表

Events in the life of Rosa Parks

February 4, 1913	Rosa Louise McCauley was born in Tuskegee, Alabama. 羅莎・路易絲・麥考利生於美國阿拉巴馬州的塔斯基吉。
1943	Rosa joined the NAACP and worked as a secretary for the local chapter. 羅莎加入全國有色人種協進會，成為蒙哥馬利分部的秘書。
December, 1955	Rosa refused to give up her seat to the white on a bus and was arrested. The bus boycott in Montgomery was launched, Rosa was convicted of breaking the bus segregation law. 羅莎因在巴士上拒向白人讓座被捕。聯合抵制蒙哥馬利巴士運動發起，羅莎被控打破了巴士種族隔離法。
1956	Rosa, King, and 86 other civil right activists were arrested for setting up the bus boycott. At the same year the Supreme Court ruled that bus segregation was unconstitutional. 因發起抵制巴士運動，羅莎、馬丁・路德・金及 86 名民權運動者被捕。同年最高法院裁定巴士種族隔離違反憲法。
1979	Rosa's mother died. Rosa won the Spingarn Medal by the NAACP and the Martin Luther King Jr. Nonviolent Peace Prize. 羅莎的母親過世。羅莎獲得全國有色人種協進會頒發的斯平加恩獎章及馬丁・路德・金非暴力和平獎。
1996	President Bill Clinton gave Rosa the Medal of Freedom. 羅莎獲克林頓總統頒發自由獎章。
1999	Rosa received the Congressional Gold Medal. 羅莎獲得國會金質獎章。
December 2000	Rosa Parks Library and Museum opened at Troy State University in Montgomery. 蒙哥馬利特洛伊大學的羅莎・帕克斯圖書館暨博物館對外開放。

2002	A movie was made about Rosa: *Ride to Freedom: The Rosa Parks Story.* 以羅莎為題材的電影拍攝完畢——《駛向自由：羅莎‧帕克斯的故事》。
2005	Rosa died at the age of ninety-two. 羅莎過世，享年九十二歲。

More to Read 延伸閱讀

Brinkley, Douglas. *Rosa Parks.* Thorndike, Maine: Thorndike Press, 2000.

King, Martin Luther, Jr. *The Words of Martin Luther King, Jr.* New York: Pocket Books, 198).

Oates, Stephen B. *Let the Trumpet Sound: The Life of Martin Luther King, Jr.* New York: Harper and Row, 1982.

Rosa Parks. *Quiet Strength.* Grand Rapids: Zondervan Publishing House, 1994.

Witherspoon, William Roger. *Martin Luther King: To the Mountaintop.* New York: Doubleday, 1985.